First published in Great Britain 2003
by Egmont Books Limited
239 Kensington High Street, London W8 6SA
Story adapted from *Harvey to the Rescue*
Photographs © Gullane (Thomas) Ltd. 2002
All Rights Reserved

Thomas the Tank Engine & Friends

A BRITT ALLCROFT COMPANY PRODUCTION

Based on The Railway Series by The Rev W Awdry

© Gullane (Thomas) LLC 2003

ISBN 1 4052 0471 0
1 3 5 7 9 10 8 6 4 2
Printed in Italy

Harvey to the Rescue

Based on *The Railway Series*
by The Rev. W. Awdry

EGMONT

An exciting new engine had arrived on the Island of Sodor. Cranky the Crane unloaded him on to the track.

"He's making my chain ache," groaned Cranky.

When the engine was unloaded, The Fat Controller introduced him.

"This is Harvey the Crane Engine," he said, proudly.

Harvey was happy to be safely on the ground. He didn't like dangling from Cranky's arm at all.

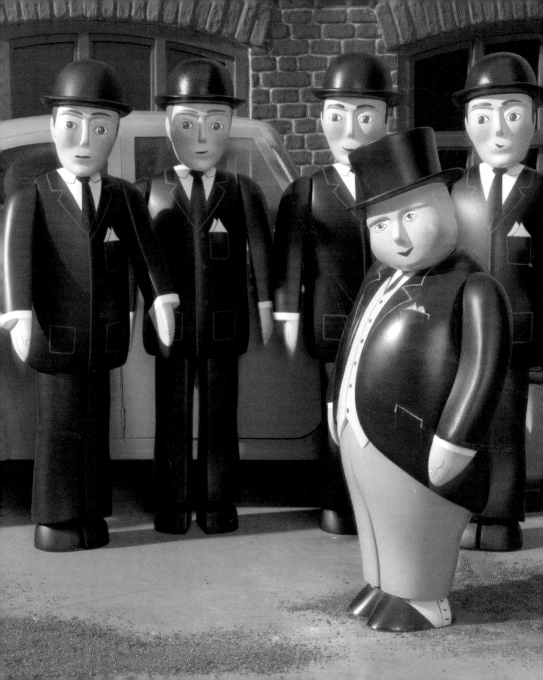

Some gentlemen were standing watching what was going on. "These are the Gentlemen of the Railway Board," The Fat Controller said. "Tomorrow Harvey will give them a demonstration. If it goes well, he will join the railway."

"What's a 'dimmer station'?" whispered
Percy to Thomas.

"Demonstration," said Thomas. "It's
when you show off what you can do."

"Like when Thomas and I have a race,"
said Bertie. "Vrooooomm! Vrooooomm!"

That evening in the engine sheds, Harvey could hear the other engines talking about him.

"Harvey's different," said Henry.

"He doesn't even look like an engine," said Edward.

Thomas felt sorry for Harvey. "Don't worry," he whispered to him.

"Sometimes it takes time to make new friends!"

But Harvey wasn't sure he wanted to stay where no one wanted him.

The next morning, Harvey said to The Fat Controller, "Maybe I shouldn't have come here, sir. The engines don't like me. I'm too different."

"Nonsense. Being different is what makes you special," The Fat Controller said.

Harvey felt a bit better after that.

Out on the branch line, Percy
was having trouble with the trucks.
"Faster we go, faster we go! Pull him
along, don't let him slow!" the trucks
chanted.

The trucks went faster and faster.
"Heeeeelp!" whistled Percy as the
Driver pulled on the brakes. But it was
too late . . .

CRASH! Percy's front wheels ran off the rails. The trucks shot off down a slope and crashed on to the road below.

That evening in the sheds, Harvey heard the engines talking about him again. But this time their talk was different.

"Isn't Harvey clever!" said Gordon.

"Very useful!" said James.

"You see," said Thomas, "different can be good!"

All the engines agreed. "Welcome to the Sodor Railway," they called.

Harvey smiled happily.